Young Billy

Young Animal Pride Series
Book 2

Cataloging-in-Publication Data

Sargent, Dave, 1941–
    Young billy / by Dave and Pat Sargent ;
illustrated by Elaine Woodward.—Prairie
Grove, AR : Ozark Publishing, c2004.
    p. cm. (Young animal pride series ; 2)

    "A new beginning"—Cover
    SUMMARY: Billy has lots of friends.
They like to play. When he is two years old
he leaves home. He must build his own lodge
and a dam.
    ISBN 1-56763-865-1 (hc)
        1-56763-866-X (pbk)

    1. Beavers—Juvenile fiction. [1. Beavers—
Fiction.] I. Sargent, Pat, 1936
II. Woodward, Elaine, 1956– ill. III. Title.
IV. Series.

    PZ10.3.S243Bi 2004
    [Fic]—dc21   2003090100

Printed in the United States of America

Young Billy

Young Animal Pride Series
Book 2

By Dave and Pat Sargent

Illustrated by Elaine Woodward

Ozark Publishing, Inc.
P.O. Box 228
Prairie Grove, AR 72753

Dave and Pat Sargent, authors of the extremely popular Animal Pride Series, plus many other Accelerated Reader books, visit schools all over the United States, free of charge. If you would like to have Dave and Pat visit your school, please ask your librarian to call 1-800-321-5671.

Foreword

Billy Beaver has lots of friends. They like to play. When he is two years old, he leaves home. He must build his own lodge and a dam.

My name is Billy.

I am a beaver.

My teeth are sharp.

I cut down trees.

5

Trees make my home.

My home is a lodge.

It is in water.

Trees make a dam.

I like Joe Frog.

We have fun.

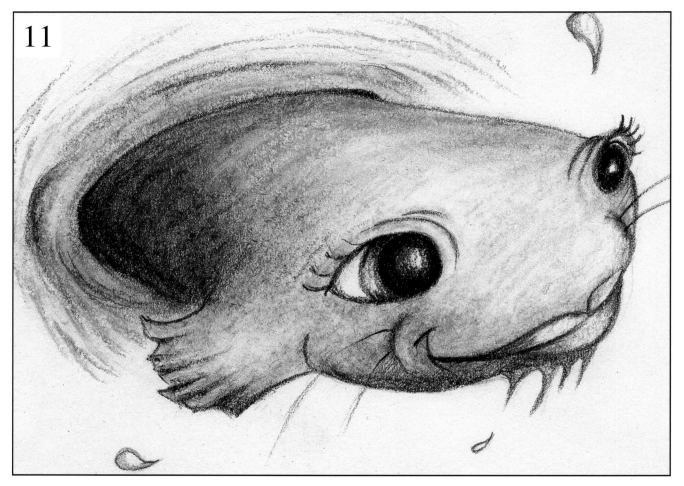

I like Sally Catfish.

She can swim fast.

I like Jack Moose.

A moose is big!

Now I am big.

I will build my lodge.

This is Suzie Beaver.

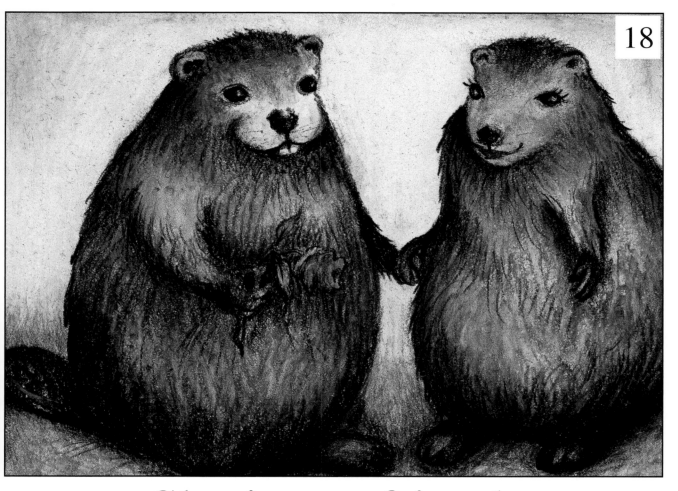

She is my friend.

Suzie will help me.